5-Minute Pout-Pout Fish Stories

Written by **Wes Adams**

Illustrated by **Isidre Monés**   Colored by **Marc Monés**

Based on the *New York Times*–bestselling Pout-Pout Fish books
written by Deborah Diesen and illustrated by Dan Hanna

Farrar Straus Giroux
New York

Farrar Straus Giroux Books for Young Readers
An imprint of Macmillan Publishing Group, LLC
120 Broadway, New York, NY 10271

Color separations by Embassy Graphics
Printed in China by RR Donnelley Asia Printing Solutions Ltd., Dongguan City, Guangdong Province
Designed by Aram Kim
First edition, 2020
10 9 8 7 6 5 4 3 2 1

mackids.com

Library of Congress Control Number: 2020904481
ISBN: 978-0-374-31400-2

Our books may be purchased in bulk for promotional,
educational, or business use. Please contact your local
bookseller or the Macmillan Corporate and
Premium Sales Department at (800) 221-7945
ext. 5442 or by email at
MacmillanSpecialMarkets@macmillan.com.

Contents

The Best Worst Day Ever   1

Trash Talk   19

Talent Show   35

The Cleanup Crew   53

Help Wanted   69

Sick Day   85

Looking for Trouble   101

Space Chase   117

Opposite Day   133

Vanishing Act   149

Cramped Quarters   165

New Adventure   177

The Best Worst Day Ever

The Pout-Pout Fish's clock tried to wake him, but he didn't want to get out of bed.

He clicked off the alarm and drifted back to slumberland.

RING!!

Oh no!
The Pout-Pout Fish woke with a start. Now it was very late.
That made him glum.

As he rushed to get ready for school, he found
his backpack hiding under a pile of dirty laundry.
That made him gloomy.

An unhappy Pout-Pout Fish gobbled his breakfast so fast he couldn't even taste it.

"*Blub, bluub, bluuub!*" he said. "Nothing is going right today."

When he darted out the door, he got lost in the hustle and
bustle of creatures zipping this way and that.

"Are you all right?" asked a little fish named Sunny who came
swishing over. She was in his class at school.

"I'm having a dreary-weary day," the Pout-Pout Fish said.

"Leave your dreary-wearies behind!" Sunny said. "If we hurry, we can still get to school on time."

"I doubt it," said the Pout-Pout Fish.

They got to school just after the bell rang.

The principal shooed them inside. "Please don't be late again tomorrow!"

The Pout-Pout Fish groaned.

"We promise!" Sunny said with a smile.

In their classroom, Miss Hewitt was saying good morning to everyone. She asked the two latecomers to put away their things and join the others on the story rug.

It was time for Morning Meeting.

"Let's talk about our day!" said Miss Hewitt.

"Let's not," grumbled the Pout-Pout Fish.

9

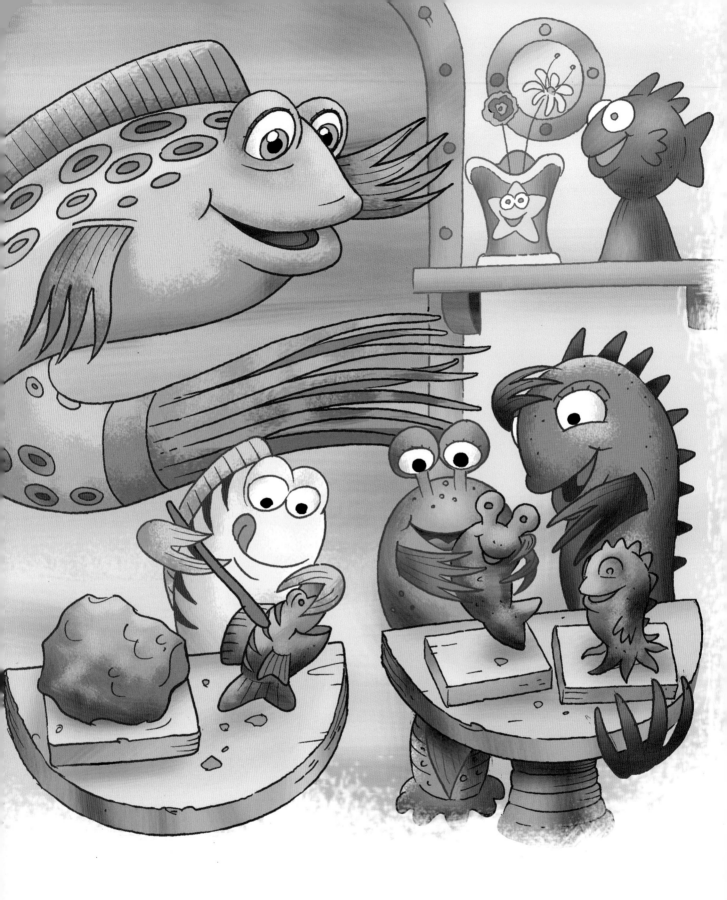

Later that morning, the class dove into a fun art project.
Miss Hewitt wanted them to make selfie sculptures.

The Pout-Pout Fish couldn't get his to look like he wanted.
"*Blub, bluub, bluuub!*" he said.
He felt like giving up.
Sunny showed him her selfie. It looked a lot like his.
"I like yours more than mine," she said with a laugh.
It seemed surprising to the Pout-Pout Fish how much she loved to laugh and smile.

At recess, Sunny's smile wavered for a moment when she bumped herself during a game.

She scraped a few scales but gave the Pout-Pout Fish a grin as he helped her up.

"Don't worry," she said. "I'm okay!"

Miss Hewitt asked Sunny to visit the nurse.
The Pout-Pout Fish said he would go with her.

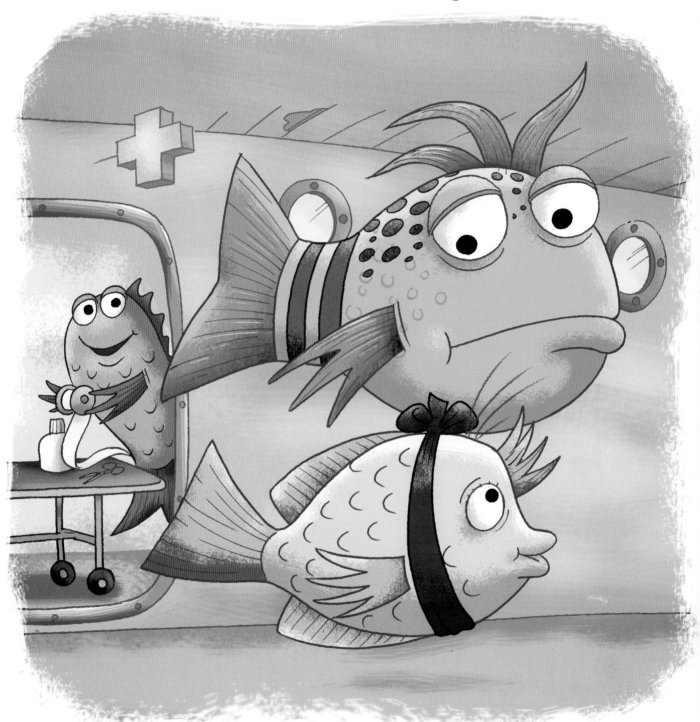

The nurse cleaned Sunny's scrapes and gave her a bright bandage.
Sunny and the Pout-Pout Fish swam back to their classroom.
"Thank you for keeping me company," she said to him.

Soon it was time for lunch.

Sunny checked her backpack and saw that her lunch sack was missing. Oh no! "It must have fallen out when we were rushing to school!" she said.

Today is just going from bad to worse, thought the Pout-Pout Fish.

But he was happy to share his food with Sunny.

Ring ring!
The school day was over. It was time to pack up and go.
"That was the worst day ever!" said the Pout-Pout Fish as
they swam home.

"For me it was the *best* worst day ever," said Sunny with a smile.
"What do you mean?" asked the Pout-Pout Fish. He reminded
her of all the things that had gone wrong. "You were late to
school, your art project looked messy, you got hurt, and you
lost your lunch sack."

"Yes, but I also found a brand-new friend," said Sunny.
The day suddenly felt a whole lot better to the grumpy,
gloomy fish. His pout turned upside down.
Sunny was right.
It was the *best* worst day ever.

Trash Talk

The Rock Bottom School Race was only a week away. The Pout-Pout Fish was training hard to get ready.

Every day, he went for a long swim. He wanted to get stronger and faster.

Every night, he went to bed early. He wanted to make sure to get lots of rest.

Shelldon was also in the race. He was in an older class. In the lunchroom, he liked to brag about his speed.

"You little slowpokes don't stand a chance," he said.

He gobbled up his food and left his trash on the table.

"Please clean up after yourself, Shelldon," said the Pout-Pout Fish. "We all have to do our share to keep our ocean home shipshape."

"Don't be so fussy," said Shelldon. "The ocean is a big place. A little trash never hurt anyone."

He swam away and left the Pout-Pout Fish to clean up after him.

The Pout-Pout Fish frowned.
He did not like Shelldon's trashy talk.
He did not like Shelldon's messy behavior.
And he did not like Shelldon calling him a slowpoke.

When race day arrived, a big crowd was gathered at the starting line.

The Pout-Pout Fish looked around. *"Blub, bluub, bluuub!"* Everyone seemed sleek and strong. He was worried.

"Ready! Set! GO!" the starter shouted.
The race was underway.
The Pout-Pout Fish found himself at the back of the pack.
Shelldon was far ahead, nowhere in sight.

The Pout-Pout Fish didn't give up. He kept swimming as fast as he could. Soon he started passing one fish after another. His hard training was paying off.

He spotted his rival way in front of the pack.

Shelldon was going strong. He looked around to see who was behind him and saw the Pout-Pout Fish.

"It's my turn to clean up today!" Shelldon taunted, not looking where he was going.

All of a sudden, Shelldon was tangled up in a pile of trash at the side of the race course.

One leg was stuck in a plastic bottle.

A claw was wrapped in a nylon net.

Shelldon was going nowhere fast.

The Pout-Pout Fish didn't think twice. He stopped to help Shelldon. In a flash, he got him untangled. Together they gathered up the garbage and took off again. The race for first place was back on!

Up ahead, the Pout-Pout Fish could see the finish.
He swam hard and sprinted his way across the line.
But he was in second place, just behind Shelldon.

Shelldon knew he couldn't have done it on his own. He gave the Pout-Pout Fish his medal.

"You deserve the prize!" he said. "Thank you for stopping to help me clean up my act."

Today, a happy Pout-Pout Fish felt like the big winner!

Talent Show

In the Pout-Pout Fish's kinderguppy class, Clara Clam loved to make her teacher and classmates laugh. Every day, she shared a new joke or riddle.

"What's slippery and shocking?" she asked during Morning Meeting. Nobody knew the answer.

"*Eel*-ectricity!"

Eli thought that was especially funny.

During recess, Clara cracked everyone up again. "How do you cut water?" she asked while they were playing among the coral.

That was a hard one. Everybody finally gave up.
"With a *sea*-saw!" Clara said.

The Pout-Pout Fish wished he were funny like Clara. He also wished he could laugh like his friend Sunny.

Sunny had a great big belly laugh that bubbled up so loud and happy it made everyone around her laugh, too.

It seemed to the Pout-Pout Fish that everyone
had a special talent.

40

Octavian made the best pictures. He could draw anything.
And with brushes, markers, and crayons in his tentacles, he was
also the fastest.

Eli told the best stories, Kai was the strongest athlete in gym class, and Finley had a way of being so calm and quiet that everyone around him felt relaxed and peaceful.

The Pout-Pout Fish didn't know what his special talent was, so he tried copying his classmates.

At Morning Meeting, he raised a fin and asked a riddle. "Why are fish so smart?"

But everyone knew the punch line.

"Because they are always in schools!" his classmates shouted.
That made the Pout-Pout Fish feel like he was very *un*-funny.

Later, when Miss Hewitt said something hilarious, he tried to make his laugh into a great big bubbly belly laugh. But it didn't come out quite right.

"Are you okay?" asked his teacher. "It sounds like you have something stuck in your throat."

The Pout-Pout Fish lost his sense of humor the rest of the morning.

In gym class, he wanted to show how fast and strong he was.
But on the agility course, he took a tumble.
That really sank his spirits.

On the way back to the classroom, he felt very sad.
His friends noticed, but nobody knew what was wrong.
Finley swam next to him calmly, and soon the Pout-Pout Fish
felt ready to talk about it.

"You are all so clever and talented," he said. One by one, he
went around the room and named his classmates' special talents.
"But I'm not especially good at anything," he said.

"Oh, that's not true at all," said Sunny. "When we are playing a game, you notice when somebody is feeling left out. You are the best noticer of us all."

"That's right," said Octavian. "You look so carefully at my pictures and always tell me how nice they are."

"When I tell stories," said Eli, "nobody is ever paying closer attention than you."

"And in gym class," added Kai, "you pay attention to what everyone is doing, and you're always cheering us on."

The Pout-Pout Fish felt so much better. Maybe his friends were right. He did love to notice all the special things his clever and talented classmates were doing. Was that his special talent?

Clara's special talent helped him know for sure.

"Well, Pout-Pout Fish," she said, "I guess this proves you have perfect eyesight."

"What do you mean?" he asked.

"Because you see things about us better than anyone!" she said.

That made everyone giggle and give a great big cheer for the Pout-Pout Fish, their clever and talented classmate—and the best noticer of them all.

The Cleanup Crew

The Pout-Pout Fish and the other kinderguppies had been busy all morning with fun games and projects. Now they were getting ready for a special picnic lunch in the rock garden at their school.

Before the Pout-Pout Fish and his classmates could leave for lunch, there was one thing left to do.

"What time is it, class?" asked Miss Hewitt.

"It's tidy-up time!" everyone answered.

"That's right," Miss Hewitt said. "And today, the Pout-Pout Fish is captain of our cleanup crew."

The Pout-Pout Fish was excited that it was his turn to be captain. He wanted to do a good job.

He made sure everyone had a task.

A few classmates grumbled, but Miss Hewitt had taught them something important. "Cleaning up," she said, "shows we care."

He helped Kai put away games. Finley and Clara returned art supplies to the cabinets.

The bookshelves needed organizing. Octavian knew just where every title belonged.

Sunny collected crayons. Eli made sure they were sharp.

After the Pout-Pout Fish checked that everybody had cleaned their tables and put away their own papers and notebooks, he decided the classroom looked shipshape.

"Starfish stickers for everyone!" Miss Hewitt said as her students swam out the door. "And two for today's captain."

At the school's picnic area, the Pout-Pout Fish was feeling proud. Even better, his special picnic basket was stuffed with all his favorite things. What a delicious meal! He and his friends had a wonderful time.

But then the Pout-Pout Fish's happy feeling vanished. He noticed that the rock garden didn't look as nice as when they'd found it.

The overflowing garbage can had tipped over. Trash was drifting here and there, tangling up in coral and piling up on rocky ledges. The sandy floor was littered with bottles and bags, cups and containers.

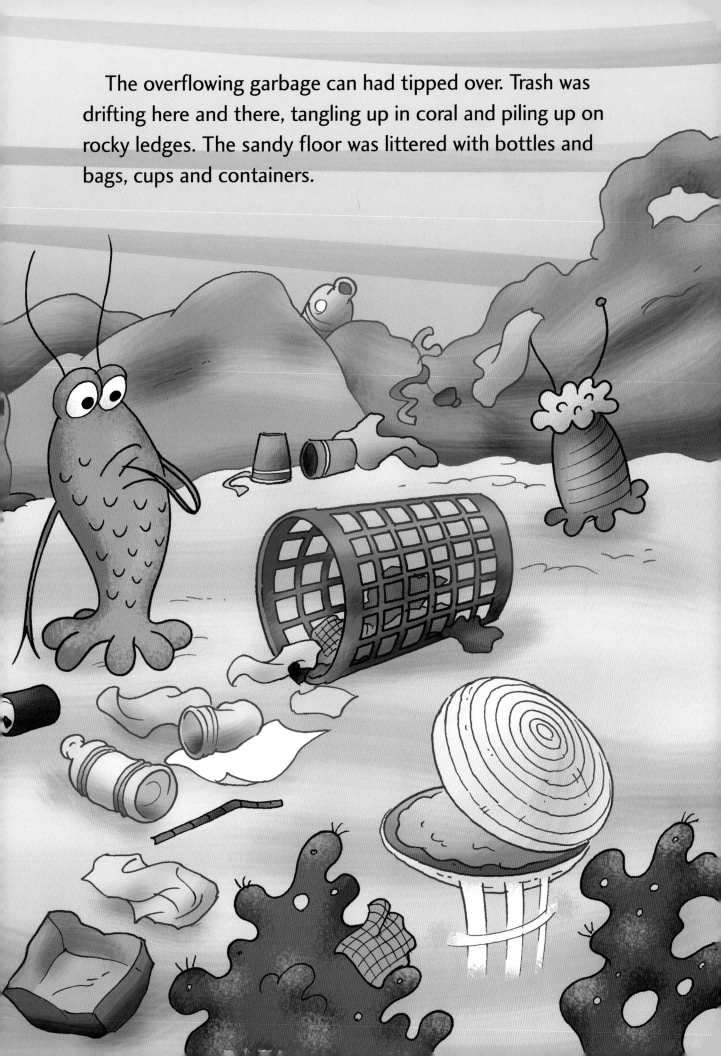

Before the kinderguppy class could leave, the cleanup crew's captain knew there was one thing left to do.

"What time is it, everyone?" he asked.

"It's tidy-up time!" everyone answered.

The class worked together to clean up the mess. As they did, they talked about how to prevent future messes. Miss Hewitt told them about the three Rs: *Reduce, Reuse,* and *Recycle.*
"Who knows what these words mean?" she asked.

"*Reduce* means to use less," said Eli.

"That's right," said their teacher. "Sometimes you don't really need what you think you need. When you do, choose things that have the least amount of packaging."

"My little seaweed snack came in this giant carton," said Finley. "It didn't need all that."

"*Reuse* means to use something again," said Kai.

"Correct you are," said Miss Hewitt. "Before you throw away a bag or a box, think about ways you might be able to use it again."

"I can make very nice bracelets out of all these straws!" said Octavian.

"*Recycle* means to put plastic and metal in separate bins," said Sunny, "where they will be taken away and converted into new kinds of plastic and metal."

"A recycle doesn't even need training wheels!" joked Clara.

PLASTIC

"Reduce, Reuse, Recycle—that's a good rule to remember!" said the Pout-Pout Fish. "And we know something else important to remember."

The kinderguppy cleanup crew smiled.

"Cleaning up," they said together, "shows we care!"

Help Wanted

One afternoon, the Pout-Pout Fish went over to his friend Sunny's house for a visit. It was the first time he had been invited to her home. He was very excited—and a little nervous. To make it a perfect playdate, he had brought something amazing to show her.

Her home was bright and colorful. Everywhere he looked, he saw something unusual. He was surprised how different it was from his cozy home on the other side of the reef.

"Would you like to work on the seashell castle I am building?"
she asked.

"Of course!" said the Pout-Pout Fish.

He had never built such a fancy model before, and he didn't
know if he could do it right. But he thought he could figure it out.

He turned out to be more like a bulldozer than a builder. His tower tipped over and broke the drawbridge. The Pout-Pout Fish felt like diving into the deep, deep dark.

"Don't worry, I can fix it later," said Sunny. "Why don't we play with something else?"

She brought out her new submarine scooter that she had gotten for her birthday.

Wow! She could zip and zoom so fast. The Pout-Pout Fish couldn't wait to try it.

"Do you know how to ride it?" asked Sunny.

Only a minnow just out of the egg doesn't know how to ride a scooter, the Pout-Pout Fish thought. He didn't want her thinking he was a baby.

"Sure!" he said.

Crash! Smash!
The Pout-Pout Fish lost control and flip-flopped.
He felt like a foolish little fry, after all.

"Maybe we should do something more relaxing," said Sunny.
"Let's make friendship bracelets."

She used the Pout-Pout Fish's favorite colors of seagrass to
braid him a handsome charm for his tail.

The Pout-Pout Fish tried his best to make one for Sunny, but all he could weave was a tangle of knots.

He was very upset. He felt like he was ruining their visit. "I don't know how to do anything!" he said.

"That's not true," said his friend.

"The only thing you don't know how to do is ask for help."

Sunny's encouraging words cheered him up. "Let me show you how to fix your bracelet," she said.

She twisted and braided until the Pout-Pout Fish understood how to do it himself. Soon, he had made a beautiful band to give his friend.

Now the Pout-Pout Fish had a question for Sunny.
"Will you teach me how to ride your scooter?"
"Of course," said Sunny.

She showed him what to do
and helped him practice.

Soon the Pout-Pout Fish was zipping around
faster than a whirlpool.

There was something else he wanted to try. "Could we rebuild the seashell castle together? You can show me how to do it."

Together they rebuilt the palace with a new tower that was straight and strong.

As he was getting ready to go home, the Pout-Pout Fish remembered that he had brought something to show his friend. It was a clever trick he had taught himself.

With Sunny looking, he covered a small pebble with an empty shell.

Then he waved a magic coral wand, and PRESTO! He revealed a big, shiny pearl.

Sunny thought it was the best trick she had ever seen. "Can you show me how to do that?"

"Of course," said the Pout-Pout Fish. "Sometimes a little help from your friend can be . . .

"MAGIC!"

Sick Day

Blub.
Blub.
Blub.
Cough!
The Pout-Pout Fish woke up with a bad cold.

As he tried to get ready for school, his head was swimming, and he ached from tip to tail. The Pout-Pout Fish knew he should stay home. He needed to rest and get better.

He put away his backpack. Then he curled up in his bed of seaweed and fell right back to sleep.

When he woke up again, staying in bed didn't seem so bad. He cuddled with his Snoozy Snuggly, and together they read their favorite book.

Then they pretended the bed was a flying ship that could shoot up out of the ocean into the skies above . . . But soon they splashed down, as the Pout-Pout Fish started to get tired and dizzy.

Blub.

   Blub.

      Blub.

         Cough!

The Pout-Pout Fish was still feeling achy, and now he was also feeling bored! He was stuck at home in his seaweed bed while all his friends were having a great time at school.

He pictured them darting into nooks and disappearing into crannies as they played an exciting game of hide-and-seek at recess.

He imagined his friends were learning all sorts of new things.
He was sure he would never catch up.

And he was missing music day! Once a week,
Miss Hewitt taught the class a bubbly new song.
The Pout-Pout Fish sank sadly down into his bed. He felt
worse than ever.

Meanwhile, the school day was not going at all how the Pout-Pout Fish was imagining. On the playground, the kinderguppies didn't play hide-and-seek. It was the Pout-Pout Fish's favorite game, and they decided it wouldn't be the same without him.

During Miss Hewitt's lessons, Octavian took careful notes so the kinderguppies' absent classmate wouldn't fall behind.

During music time, they didn't feel much like singing. It just wasn't the same without the Pout-Pout Fish. But then Miss Hewitt helped them invent a new song: a song about how much they missed their glum-faced chum.

After school, a group of kinderguppies swam off. They were on a mission.

The Pout-Pout Fish was surprised to see his friends. He was even more surprised to hear the song they sang for him:

Dear Pout-Pout Fish,
When you are out-out sick,
All of us have one-one wish:
GET WELL AND COME BACK-BACK QUICK!

The sweet and silly song made him feel much, much better. After saying goodbye to his friends, the Pout-Pout Fish got comfy and cozy in his seaweed bed. Even though he'd missed school, he had learned something new: Friendship is the best medicine!

Looking for Trouble

One afternoon, the Pout-Pout Fish was swimming around with some of his friends.

"Let's play tag," said Sunny. "I'm not it!"

"Not it!" cried everyone except the Pout-Pout Fish. He didn't mind being it to get the game started.

Soon, he regretted being such a good sport. He could not catch anyone. Either his friends were extra speedy, or he was extra slow today.

This game is no good, he thought. Just then,
Stefie and Clara darted right in front of him.
"Can't catch me!" said the squid.
"Can't catch me!" said the clam.

The Pout-Pout Fish dove but missed them both.
Instead, he scraped his tail.
"Ouch!" he shouted.

His friends paused the game to make sure he was okay.
It wasn't a big scrape. After a few trembles and tears,
the Pout-Pout Fish was feeling fine.

"Be careful, Pout-Pout Fish!" said Stefie and Clara.
"Let's play. I will be it now," said Sunny.

106

With shouts and squeals, everyone darted away.

The Pout-Pout Fish scooted off with Flo and Ray, two very slithery sea creatures who'd joined the fun. As Sunny came closer, the Pout-Pout Fish tried to slip under a ledge with them and bumped his nose.

"Stop the game," said Flo.

"Pout-Pout Fish is hurt again," said Ray.

"You keep finding trouble," said Stefie.

"Maybe you need a break," said Clara.

The Pout-Pout Fish's frown was bigger than ever.

It wasn't a bad bump, but he decided Clara was right.

"Stay right here," said Ray. "Don't flick a flipper."
"It's for your own good, Pout-Pout Fish. You don't know what could happen next," said Clara.

The Pout-Pout Fish sighed a big burst of bubbles. He was going to miss out on the rest of the game.

But his friend Sunny knew what he was thinking.

"We won't play tag without you," she said. "We'll stay right here and keep you safe."

Everyone agreed with Sunny. They didn't want their friend to have any more troubles.

That made the Pout-Pout Fish feel better. And after swimming all around, it was nice to sit and take it easy with his friends.

At first, all of them chatted and told stories and jokes. But soon, they ran out of things to say. They grew quiet. Many of them fell fast asleep.

The Pout-Pout Fish felt very safe—and very bored. And then he realized something. "Oh no!" he said.

"What's wrong?" asked Sunny.

"I am fine," said the Pout-Pout Fish. "But sitting around and waiting for something terrible to happen when we should be playing and having fun is no good."

"It is worse than a scrape on your fin or a bump on your nose."
The Pout-Pout Fish darted off. "Let's play tag," he said. "And
I am *not* it!"

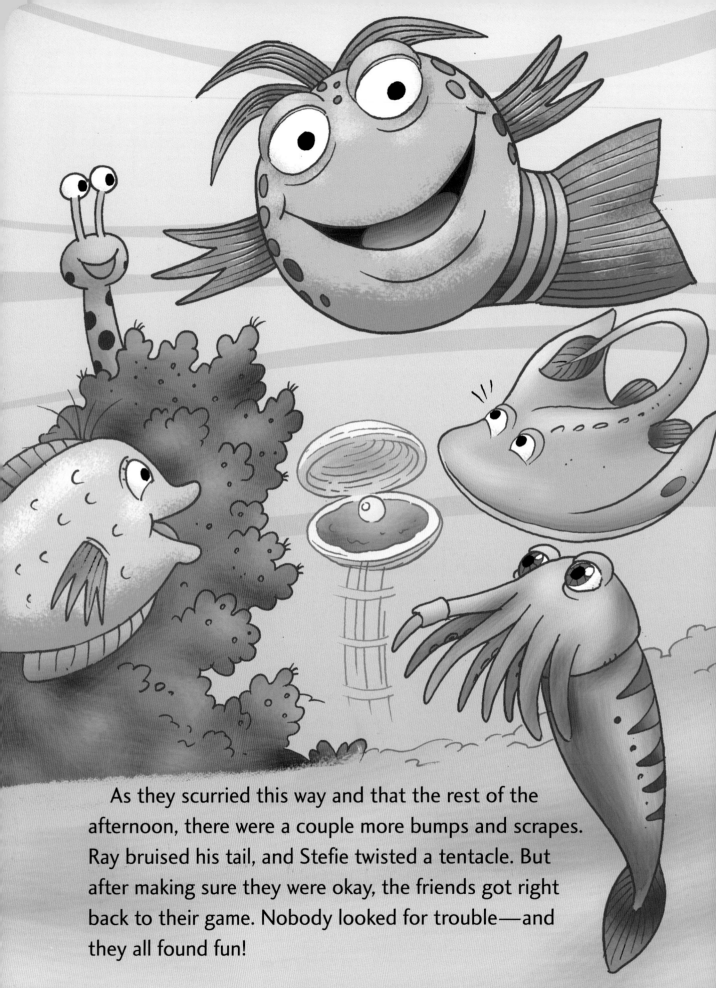

As they scurried this way and that the rest of the afternoon, there were a couple more bumps and scrapes. Ray bruised his tail, and Stefie twisted a tentacle. But after making sure they were okay, the friends got right back to their game. Nobody looked for trouble—and they all found fun!

Space Chase

One morning, Miss Hewitt announced that the kinderguppy class was launching a special mission.

"You mean like a rocket ship?" asked the Pout-Pout Fish.

Their teacher smiled. "I mean that today, we are going to explore the wonders of outer space. Each of you will choose a space topic to report on in front of the class."

"That will be out of this world!" said Eli.

"Too far!" said Stefie. "What does outer space have to do with the ocean?"

"Why don't we find out?" said their teacher. "Five, four, three, two, one . . . Let the space chase begin."

Blast off! Everyone rushed to pick an interesting topic.
"I choose the planets in our solar system," said Octavian,
who loved to handle more than one thing at a time.

"I bet Sunny chooses the sun," said Clara.

"She can choose whatever subject she wants," said Miss Hewitt.

"Where would we be without everyone's favorite star?" Sunny asked. "I am happy to learn more about it."

As his classmates settled on their choices, the Pout-Pout Fish imagined flying up, up, up—out of the ocean, through the blue skies, and into the darkness above. Rocketing into space seemed a lot like diving down into the big, big dark.

For his topic, the Pout-Pout Fish decided to stay close to home. He chose the moon. Miss Hewitt said it seemed like a very good choice.

Miss Hewitt helped all the students find classroom library books filled with pictures and information about their topics. The Pout-Pout Fish discovered two books about the moon to read and explore.

The students all worked hard on their presentations. They read and drew. They cut out props and practiced what they were going to say.

124

Finally, it was time for their space mission to begin. Miss Hewitt let them choose the order in which the students would present their space topic. The Pout-Pout Fish was last, and Octavian went first.

"There are eight planets in our solar system," the octopus said, holding a model of each planet in his tentacles. "They all circle the sun. But Earth is the only planet with water where we can live."

He wowed them with many more facts about the planets.

Stefie talked about pictures in the sky known as constellations. "They are formed by drawing imaginary lines between certain stars. Many constellations are pictures of sea creatures such as a crab, a whale, and a porpoise. One of the best known is Pisces, a constellation of two fish!"

"Why are there no clam constellations?" asked Clara.

The Pout-Pout Fish laughed even though he was starting to feel nervous about getting up in front of the class.

One by one, other students took their turn.

Sunny talked about how the sun's light feeds the ocean plants that many sea creatures eat. "Heat from the sun also helps cause waves and currents, and it keeps our water the right temperature."

127

Eli blew them away by talking about flying objects called asteroids. "An asteroid is a big rock in the sky that blasts through space faster than you can imagine. Sixty-six million years ago, a giant asteroid the size of a mountain hit the ocean. Ash and dust from the impact blocked sunlight, causing the planet to cool down and ice to cover parts of the earth."

The Pout-Pout Fish shivered, but it wasn't from hearing about the cold. It was his turn next. *You can do this*, he told himself.

"You might think the moon is just another big rock in the sky," the Pout-Pout Fish began. "But it is so much more. As it circles our planet, the moon causes an invisible force to make the ocean's tides go up and down."

"That sounds like magic," said Clara.

"That sounds like a force called gravity," said Miss Hewitt.

The Pout-Pout Fish amazed his classmates with more moon facts. "The moon looks like it is covered with land and seas," he said.

"Far out!" said Eli. "Let's all move to the moon!"

"But there's no water on the moon," the Pout-Pout Fish added. "What we see when we look at the moon are dry plains and basins."

"The moon is our night-light. When our part of the earth is turned away from the sun at night, the sun sneaks us a little light by bouncing it off the moon and down to us." The Pout-Pout Fish smiled at his friend Sunny. "The sunshine helps us see the moon. And I think it helps the moon feel less alone in the dark."

Miss Hewitt said it was the perfect ending to the kinderguppies' exciting day—and when she sent them outside for recess, a proud Pout-Pout Fish had one more thing to say to all his fellow explorers.

"Let the space chase begin!"

Opposite Day

One morning, the Pout-Pout Fish met his friends Eli and Octavian at the park. He was the last to arrive.

"It's awful to see you," said Eli with a great big smile.

"That's not nice," said the Pout-Pout Fish.

Eli laughed. "Turn your pout inside out. I mean I'm happy
to see you. We've decided that today is Opposite Day.
So we're saying the opposite of what we mean."

"*Up* means *down*. And *big* means *small*," said Octavian.

"Oh," said the Pout-Pout Fish. "I can't play that game."
"Why not?" asked Eli. "It's just—"
"I think he has already started playing," said Octavian.
"I get it!" said Eli, and they all laughed.

"Let's not build a sandcastle," said the Pout-Pout Fish.

"Let's each not build one," said Eli as he and Octavian got busy. "Mine will be the smallest one of all."

"We'll see," said Octavian.

The Pout-Pout Fish worked hard on his castle. He made giant walls and tall turrets, and he liked what he'd done. He was sure his castle would be the opposite of the smallest one of all.

But when he looked around, he saw that his castle wasn't as big and grand as the others.

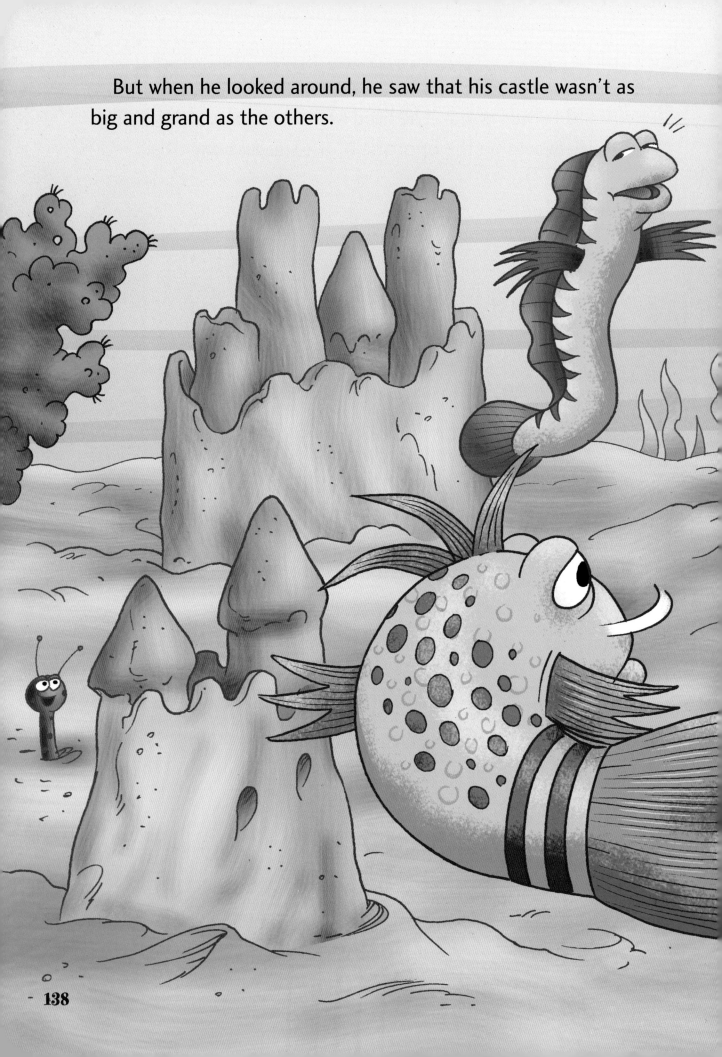

"My castle is the tiniest!" said Octavian.

"Of course it is," huffed Eli. "You have so few tentacles, and that makes it harder for you."

The Pout-Pout Fish didn't want to squabble. "Let's do something else," he suggested.

"You mean let's do nothing," said Octavian in opposite talk.

"I know!" said Eli. "Let's clean up our castles."
He charged straight into his, knocking it over
and messing it all up.

It looked like so much fun, the other two did the same with their castles.

Then the Pout-Pout Fish said he wanted to show his two friends a not-special place he'd found the other day. "It's very ugly," he promised as they traveled across the seabed.

"Wow!" said Octavian.

"It's the ugliest thing I've ever seen," said Eli, amazed at the secluded reef's beauty.

Then the Pout-Pout Fish spotted something he hadn't noticed before.

"Don't look here!" he said. "It's not the entrance to a cave."
The three of them peeked inside.
"We definitely shouldn't explore that," Eli said. "It looks very uninteresting."
"You're right," said Octavian. "I mean, you're wrong."
The octopus slipped inside and disappeared.

The other two followed. Even when his eyes got used to
the gloom, the Pout-Pout Fish couldn't see much.

"This is . . . fun," he said, when he was definitely feeling
the opposite.

Octavian scooted around a corner. "Stay away!" he called.

His two friends followed, swimming deeper into the dark.

After going up one passage and down another, the Pout-Pout Fish felt all turned around.

"I think we might be lost," he said.

"I hope you mean we're not lost," said Eli.

"No, we're definitely lost," said Octavian.

The Pout-Pout Fish didn't understand what anybody was saying! "I'm declaring an end to Opposite Day. I'm worried that we might be lost."

"Oh no!" said Eli. "I was saying I hope you were saying we were not lost."

"And I was saying that we are definitely not lost," said Octavian. "I know the way out!"

Octavian was right. He did know the way out. He led them out of the dark and gloomy place.

"What a relief to be back at the reef," said Eli.

"It sure is awful—I mean wonderful—to be safe and sound with you," said the Pout-Pout Fish, glad that Opposite Day was over and positive that he was saying exactly what he meant!

Vanishing Act

One afternoon at recess, the Pout-Pout Fish saw Sunny swim off to a corner of the playground all by herself. She seemed sad. He hadn't seen her smile all day. It was time to cheer up his friend, and he knew just how to do it.

The Pout-Pout Fish had been practicing a new magic trick. "Look, Sunny," he said. "I can make a coin disappear in my special hat." He picked up one of the many gold doubloons scattered on the seafloor around their shipwreck school. Then he dropped it into his upside-down hat and said, "Abracadabra!"

The Pout-Pout Fish turned his hat over. Nothing fell out. "The coin is gone!" he said proudly. "I bet you didn't think I could make something vanish."

Sunny did not say a word. Instead, she looked even sadder and swam away.

Miss Hewitt drifted over. "What's happening here?" she asked.

The Pout-Pout Fish told her that his coin trick had upset Sunny instead of cheering her up.

"I'm sure that's not right, but let me go talk to her," said the teacher.

Kai and Eli stopped their game of chase and wanted to know what was going on.

"Are you and Sunny having an argument?" Kai asked.

"No," said the Pout-Pout Fish. "But something is upsetting her."

Clara was having a pretend picnic with Stefie. "Maybe she ate too much at lunch today and has a bellyache."

The squid disagreed. "I think she ate too little and is feeling light-headed."

Octavian closed all the books he had been reading and said he knew what might be bothering Sunny. "Sometimes we have a pop quiz after recess. Maybe she is worried about not knowing the right answers."

The Pout-Pout Fish wished he knew the right answer about his friend.

While the other kinderguppies were talking, Sunny told her teacher what was bothering her. She was moving away with her family. Miss Hewitt listened as Sunny talked about the move and the feelings she was having about it. After Miss Hewitt gave her a big hug, she asked Sunny if she was ready to share the news with her classmates.

Sunny said yes, and their teacher called everyone over. In a quiet voice, Sunny announced that she was moving away to a new home. "I'm excited about it, but I'm also sad, because I'll be leaving this class," she said. Everyone was very upset when they heard the news. Nobody wanted their friend Sunny to leave.

Miss Hewitt asked all her sad students to settle down in a circle. She said she would tell them a story. "Once upon a time, I was a small fry in a class like this one. One of my best friends was a crab named Lola. She was the nicest sea creature I had ever met. She had sharp claws, but she was so gentle and kind.

"Lola and I loved to play school together. She always let me be the teacher. She said I did such a good job and that she knew I would become a wonderful teacher when I grew up."

"One day, Lola had to move to a new undersea home far away. Even though we might visit sometimes, it was hard to say goodbye. But after she left, I realized my friend had not really gone. None of the kind things she had done for me had disappeared. I remembered them all. And even now, as I get ready for each and every school day, I think of her telling me that I would be a wonderful teacher."

As he listened to Miss Hewitt's story, the Pout-Pout Fish understood why his magic trick had upset his friend. He had made something disappear at a time Sunny was feeling sad about going away. She was afraid their friendship would disappear!

He picked up his hat and swam over to show it to her. The gold coin was inside, hidden in a secret compartment. He had not made it vanish. "My magic is just pretend," he said to Sunny. "Your friendship is the real magic for us all."

The other kinderguppies agreed. One by one, they each said something about Sunny that they admired or appreciated.
Kai said she was very good at tag.

Octavian said she was smart and always knew the right answers. Eli thanked her for sharing her lunch with him once or twice and asked if she had any lunch left to share today, because he was hungry. That was when the Pout-Pout Fish heard the sound of Sunny's laugh—for the first time all day.

It was a sound he knew he would never forget, and something
that would never, ever vanish, even after they said goodbye.
And he also knew he was a great letter writer!

Cramped Quarters

One morning, the Pout-Pout Fish sprang out of his seaweed bed and bumped his tail on the table. Ouch! Then he stubbed his fin against a wall. Oof!

The Pout-Pout Fish looked all around him. What a cramped, uncomfortable place it was! "This home is too small," he said to his Snoozy Snuggly. "I wish we had a big new house."

A distant rumble interrupted his daydream. Above the ocean surface, a storm was raging. Thunder crashed. Lightning flashed. As fierce winds blew and giant waves churned, a strong current swept deep under the surface. It lifted silt off the ocean floor and made it hard to see. It pushed aside anyone in its way.

The Pout-Pout Fish heard someone at his door.

It was Octavian. "Can I come in out of this chaotic current?" he asked. "I am losing my grip on things."

"Of course!" said the Pout-Pout Fish. "But be careful. It's a little cramped in here."

"Not at all," said Octavian, settling in a corner. "I'm used to
much tighter spaces."

The Pout-Pout Fish was fixing a snack for his visitor when
he heard another voice at his door. Actually, it was another
two voices.

It was Ray and Flo, his stingray and flounder friends.

"Hi!" said Ray. "The water is wild today."

"Hey!" said Flo. "Would you mind if we sheltered with you for a bit?"

"Of course not," said the Pout-Pout Fish. "If you can squeeze in."

As the Pout-Pout Fish wondered how he could ever be a good host in such a small space, he heard more voices outside his door. *Many* more voices!

Kai had been out shopping, and the heavy current had nearly swept him off into the deep, deep dark. An elderly turtle was finding swimming a struggle. A squad of sea snakes was all turned around and tangled up.

The Pout-Pout Fish urged everyone to come in and make themselves as comfortable as they could. As he swished this way and that to take care of them, he got too busy to worry about how cramped and crowded his little place was.

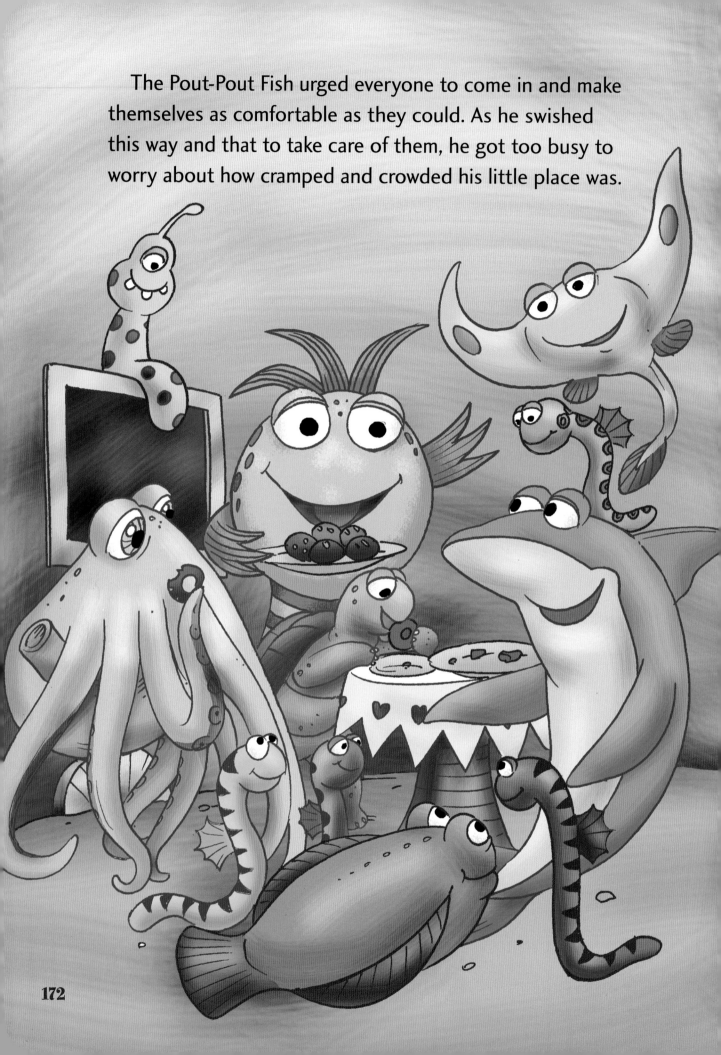

Outside, the storm current surged. Inside, everyone's spirits rose. They sang silly songs in loud voices. They played games that brought on shouts and laughs. It became an unexpected party—and the visitors insisted their host was the fish of honor. They all thanked him for taking care of them. They were so grateful.

Gradually, the storm passed, and the crazy current settled down. Ray and Flo were the first to leave, followed by Octavian waving goodbye.

Then the sea snakes slithered out, and Kai said he would escort the old sea turtle home. Now it was just the Pout-Pout Fish and his Snoozy Snuggly.

The Pout-Pout Fish looked all around him. What a roomy, comfortable place it was! "This home is just right," he said to his Snoozy Snuggly.

The Pout-Pout Fish was so happy. He couldn't imagine living anywhere else!

New Adventure

It was Day One Hundred of the school year, and the kinderguppies were ready to celebrate being together for such a long time.

Finley had decorated himself with one hundred polka dots. Kai, Clara, Stefie, and Eli had each brought twenty-five healthy snacks to share, because they knew that twenty-five plus twenty-five plus twenty-five plus twenty-five equals one hundred.

But the Pout-Pout Fish knew that for one newcomer, it was only Day One. Their teacher had told them that a seahorse named Sam would be joining the kinderguppies today.

He spotted her in the hallway. She looked scared, as if the classroom were a haunted house filled with ghouls and goblins.

She bravely made her way through the door. But then she darted into a corner, looking for a place to hide.

The Pout-Pout Fish thought Sam might need a friend.
"Hello," he said. "This is a good secret spot. Would you
mind if I joined you?"
Sam smiled shyly and made room for him.

Peeping out, they watched all the other kinderguppies arrive and gather around the teacher.

"That's Miss Hewitt," the Pout-Pout Fish told Sam. "It is time for Morning Meeting."

"At my old school, we called it Circle Time, not Morning Meeting," she said.

"I wonder what other differences you will discover today," the Pout-Pout Fish said. "Do you want to come sit next to me?"

Sam gave a grateful nod, and they swam together to join the others.

Miss Hewitt smiled at Sam and said, "Good morning, everyone. We have had so many adventures together in our first one hundred days, and today, a new adventure begins."

"Are we going on a field trip?" asked Octavian the octopus.

"No," the teacher said. "Today, we are starting an adventure with a new classmate." She introduced the seahorse, and everyone said hello.

For Sam, the new adventure was filled with highs and lows.

During a math lesson, she and her friend used one hundred blocks to make a tall tower.

It was just as fun to clean them all up when it tipped over.

But at recess, she discovered that the playground slide seemed too steep and curvy.

"Don't worry," the Pout-Pout Fish said. "You will slide down when you are ready."

During a yoga lesson, the seahorse didn't know any of the positions.

"Downward dogfish is my favorite," the Pout-Pout Fish said as he showed her how to do it.

For an art project, Miss Hewitt asked everyone to draw a picture of one of their classmates.

"I'm going to make a picture of you," the Pout-Pout Fish told Sam.

Sam laughed. "I'm going to make a picture of you," she said.

When art time was over, the teacher asked everyone to write their partner's name under their picture and give it to them. Suddenly, Sam looked very upset. She scooted away, back to her hiding place.

The Pout-Pout Fish wondered if she did not like his picture.

This time, her hiding place was no secret. Her new classmates gathered around.

"What's wrong?" asked Octavian. "Was your Day One not fun?"

Sam said it had been amazing. "Each of you gave me one hundred reasons to feel welcome, and one of you most of all . . . But I feel embarrassed, because I forgot to ask him his name."

"Oh, we know just who you mean," said Clara.
"He's a fin-tastic fellow," said Eli.
"He's one of a kind!" said Kai.
"He's the Pout-Pout Fish!" everyone shouted, and then they gave a big cheer.

"It's a wonderful picture," said the Pout-Pout Fish.

"And you're a wonderful friend," said Sam.

The Pout-Pout Fish smiled, feeling grateful for all his friends: new and old, near and far, underwater and above the ocean—including *you*!